ACTION MAN FILES™

JOHN MICHLIG

WATSON-GUPTILL PUBLICATIONS / NEW YORK

"This is Nick Masters, coming to you live from the MasterDome where Alex Mann, the Action Man, is moments away from winning yet another event in the Acceleration Games! The full-pipe/half-pipe course is being shredded!"

Alex rode his board down the supersteep slopes and into tight curls with ease. In his earpiece radio, he could hear advice from the members of his squad, Team Xtreme.

"You're way ahead of everyone, buddy," said Rikki, the Team's business manager. "Just make sure the camera can get some nice shots of our logo so the sponsors will be happy!"

"No prob," Alex answered as he went airborne from one concrete ramp to another. "Just have a nice cool lemonade ready for me at the finish line."

"Can do!" answered Fidget, the Team's cameraperson. She was tracking Alex on her remote camera.

Suddenly a strange voice broke through the radio transmission. "Look out behind you!" It said. Surprised, Alex swung his head around to see . . . nothing!

"Who was that?" Grinder, the Team's mechanical whiz, exclaimed. "Who's on our locked frequency?"

Alex wheeled his head back around—just in time to see a rolling obstacle coming right at him!

"Uh-oh, it looks like Alex Mann has miscalculated one of our track hazards and is heading for a wipeout!" announced Nick Masters.

"Whoa!" Alex thought. "Time to *check it out, dial it in, and amp it up!*"

Suddenly, Alex could see time stop in front of him. Angles and mathematical equations played out over the scene. His AMP Factor was kicking in!

He could see every possible action and every possible result and choose the very one that would work perfectly. Moving in an instant, he leapt off the board.

Nick Masters breathlessly described the scene. "The Action Man is living up to his name! He's launched himself over the obstacle, and it looks like—YES! He's met his board on the other side and has crossed the finish line!"

"What just happened?!" Fidget exclaimed.

"Hey, a win's a win," Rikki said,"but that one goes on the highlight reel!"

"Wow, I really didn't see that coming," Alex told the Team as he skidded to a halt. "Did anyone else hear a strange voice on the radio?"

They all nodded. "The Team Xtreme radio frequency is top secret," Grinder said. "In order for someone to get it, they would have to have access to our computer files—but that's impossible. . . ."

"Until we figure out who that was, we'll have to stay out of competition," Alex said. "Something like this puts us all in danger."

"Who's going to tell Nick Masters we're going to take a break?" Rikki asked. "He's not going to be happy—you're the star of his games!"

"It'll be less painful if we do it together," Alex replied.

The Team arrived in Nick Masters's giant office atop the MasterDome.

"Congratulations on your win!" Masters said as he greeted his guests. "I thought you'd lose it, though. What happened?"

"Someone broke into our frequency during the event," Alex said. "It looks like we'll have to bow out for a while so can find out who's behind it. I think our crime-fighting work has made us an enemy or two."

Masters was angry. "Bow out for a while? What am I supposed to tell your fans? And what about my sponsors? You're paid to be an athlete, not a superhero. This little crime-fighting hobby of yours is going to ruin my ratings!"

"Little hobby?!" Fidget asked angrily.

"You heard me," Masters answered. "Now you'll have to excuse me. I have a network to run."

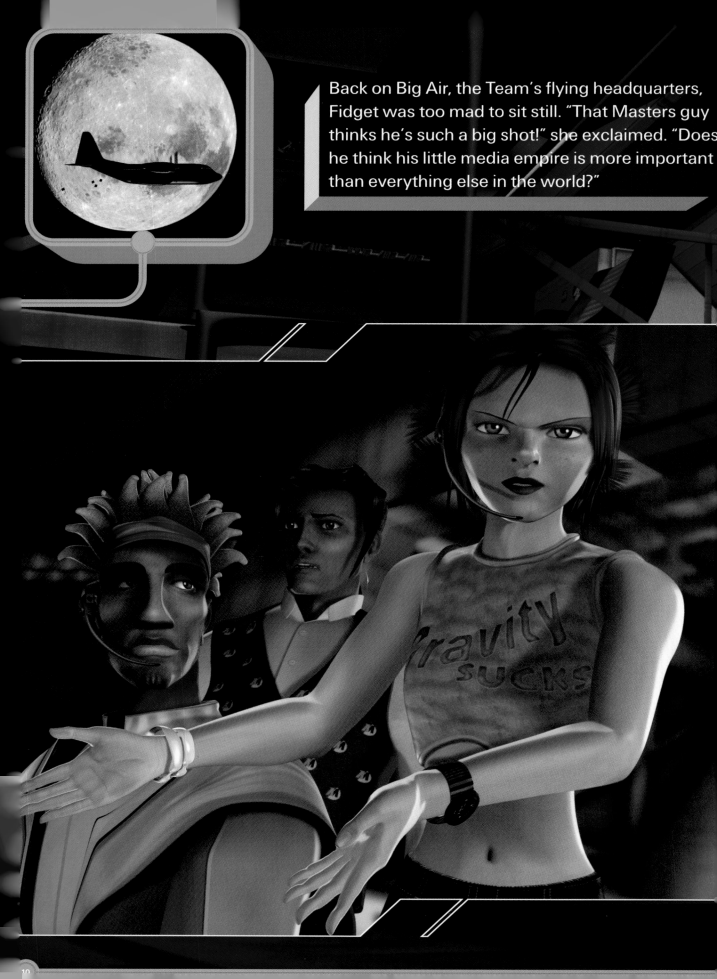

Back on Big Air, the Team's flying headquarters, Fidget was too mad to sit still. "That Masters guy thinks he's such a big shot!" she exclaimed. "Does he think his little media empire is more important than everything else in the world?"

"Well," Rikki answered, "his little media empire and the exposure it gives Team Xtreme go a long way toward paying the bills around here. Don't forget that saving the world can be pretty tough if you can't afford to gas up the jet."

"If you want something to worry about," Grinder said from his seat in front of the computer, "how about that strange voice that broke into our secure radio frequency? The only way to do that is by getting into our computer files—and I don't like what I see here."

"I've built some nasty alarms into our secure files, and it looks like someone or something got into our database," Grinder explained as the Team gathered around his computer. "See the red warning light at the top right? That means someone has broken into this file!"

WELCOME

 **WARNING!**

TEAM USER

PASSWORD

●●●●●●●●●●

"So someone can read our computer files?" Alex asked.

"It's possible," Grinder answered. "Whoever this is, they're smart—and they might find a way into our top secret files!"

"This is a disaster!" a worried Rikki chimed in. "What if our sponsors find out?"

"Our sponsors?!" Fidget exclaimed. "What about our guy, Alex? He almost wiped it big time back there because of some hacker!"

"Well, er, that's the point," Rikki replied. "It's not easy to keep our funding if we lose our star."

"I'm touched by your concern, Rikki," Alex said with a smile.

Fidget sat in front of another computer terminal. "It's pretty obvious to me who's behind this mess," she said. "It's as plain as the gel in Rikki's hair!"

"Our Fidget, the detective," Rikki sighed. "When she's not pulling pranks, she's solving mysteries."

With a few keystrokes, Fidget had their file for Nick Masters up on her screen.

NICK MASTERS

Nick Masters owns MasterVision Broadcasting and the Acceleration Games circuit. He appears on TV as master of ceremonies, and will pursue high ratings at any cost.

Masters calls himself the "King of Media." He is boastful and greedy, but not a threat to national security.

Masters also wears one of the worst wigs I've ever seen! It gets pretty obvious when you fly a helicopter right over his head, which I try to do as much as possible.

MASTERDOME

The MASTERDOME is the huge state-of-the-art sports dome where the Acceleration Games events take place. It can hold thousands of fans. A giant video screen provides up-close views of the athletes. The playing field can quickly change into different environments for a wide range of events.

ACCELERATION GAMES EVENTS

Wingboarding

Active Volcano
Skysurfing

Sailboard Cyclone
Circuit

Grapple Biking

Urban Subterranean
Thrash

Full-Pipe
Half-Pipe

Urban Sport
Climbing

Human Pinball
Biathlon

SnowEagling

Rikki wasn't convinced. "Masters is a smart businessman," he said, "and Alex is his star attraction. What would he have to gain from tripping him up?"

"Rikki's right," Alex added. "As much as you like to think he's always the bad guy, Masters would have a hard time getting top athletes to do his Acceleration Games if they thought things could go wrong."

Grinder nodded. "Yeah, dude. And besides, check it out—his file was tampered with, too, so it can't be him. Scratch him off the list of suspects."

"Well, what about our files?" asked Fidget. "Does this mean some weirdo knows all about me? Creepy!"

With a few keystrokes, Grinder had the Team Xtreme file up on his screen.

TEAM XTREME

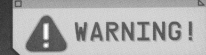

Team Xtreme consists of ALEX MANN and his support staff: DESMOND "GRINDER" SINCLAIR, FIDGET WILSON, and RIKKI PATEL.

Team Xtreme was brought together to compete in Nick Masters' Acceleration Games. They travel in a modified military airplane known as BIG AIR. This also acts as their headquarters.

The recent discovery of Alex Mann's extraordinary powers (known as the AMP FACTOR) has caused the Team to become involved in various crime-fighting adventures, guided by the mysterious SIMON GREY.

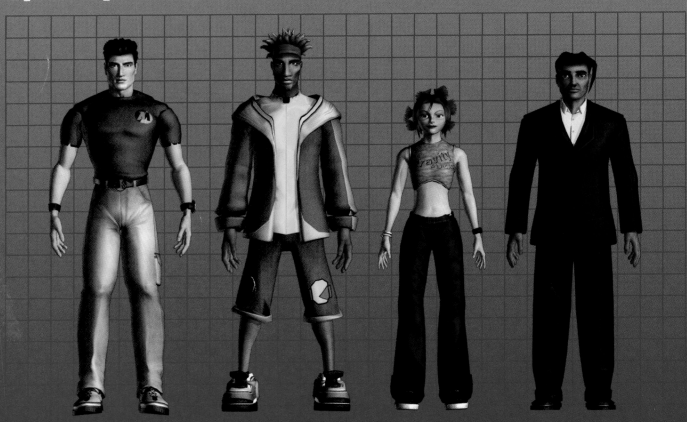

"I gotta think the hacker would have tried to see Alex's files right away," Fidget said. "After all, he's the star of the show—and he's the guy with the weird 'amp it up' thing that everybody wants to figure out."

"The AMP Factor," Alex corrected. "But you're right—it is weird."

"That's a good idea," Grinder said. "I bet there's a whole waiting list of other teams trying to learn how Alex does that . . . thing."

"Well, I'm still trying to learn how I do it, too!" Alex laughed.

ALEX MANN

Alex Mann, also known as "Action Man," was into extreme sports long before he discovered his strange abilities. He's among the most popular of all competitors in the Acceleration Games circuit, and spends a lot of time in the winner's circle. Alex has a sense of humor and is known to play a practical joke or two on his teammates.

Alex's family background is a mystery, but his Xtreme Teammates seem to form a close unit that he can rely on for support.

"Action Man" was my idea. Has a nice ring to it and it's great marketing!

It's pretty hard to faze Alex. He's such an easygoing guy. But if you want to make him blush, go ahead and call him "Action Man." He thinks it's a pretty silly nickname!

MISSION XTREME WATCH

The Mission Xtreme Watch can do almost anything. It even tells Alex which buttons to push, which is pretty handy since Alex never reads instruction manuals!

The Mission Xtreme Watch is a multi-purpose personal communications device. Computer discs can be inserted to turn it into a pager, Global Positioning System Tracker, personal database, and communicator as needed. Grinder is always adding new abilities to it.

The Advanced Macro-Probability (AMP) Factor is a mysterious power within extreme athlete ALEX MANN. He has only recently learned how to control it.

The AMP Factor is based on the AMP Equation, a math formula that was designed by a group of doctors and scientists known as PROJECT PHOENIX. Their goal was to create a better human race. The AMP Equation was designed to allow a person to predict the future by seeing all possible results of any action.

Some in Project Phoenix believed that they could give a person this ability if trained at an early age. As a test, they did a secret experiment at a school. They used the school's PA system to play music filled with secret messages meant to create the AMP Equation in students without them knowing it. It was thought that their experiment had failed until one of the children, Alex Mann, began showing AMP Factor abilities many years later.

I didn't know what was happening to me at first! I'm told that "AMP" stands for Advanced Macro-Probability, but to me it means that time sort of slows down when I'm in a tight situation. It's as if everything stops and I can see each possible result of every action imaginable. I'm still learning how to control it with the help of Simon Grey and Project Phoenix.

"That's a relief," Grinder said. "No one's been able to get past my security into Alex's files. The old Grinder magic has them locked up tight."

"Grinder magic or not, let's check them all out," Alex suggested. "Everybody check your own files first and go from there."

"A good idea," Fidget said. "Let's get to it!"

FIDGET WILSON

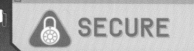

🔒 SECURE

Fidget is Team Xtreme's photographer and documentarian. The youngest member of the Team, she is a thrill-seeker who sometimes has problems dealing with authority. Fidget's ability to forget danger and get the perfect shot has contributed greatly to the success of the Team.

 Problem with authority? Who says I have a problem with authority? And who writes these things, anyway? I'll bet it's Rikki....

VINNIE

TEAM MASCOT

DESMOND GRINDER SINCLAIR

His motto: "Can't be done. When do you need it?"

Grinder was born in the Caribbean and raised in the U.K. He is Team Xtreme's mechanical and technological magician. If there's a machine or computer that he can't fix, improve, or soup up, he hasn't seen it yet. He can make something out of anything, and he saves every scrap of machinery he finds.

Grinder is always cool under pressure. It's almost as though he is without fear. He also likes to say strange things like "No guts, no shoes, no service."

Grinder's relationship with Alex Mann goes back before Team Xtreme. In fact, it was Grinder who brought Alex into the world of extreme sports.

Between his technobabble and weird statements like "The devil's in the detours," it's like Grinder speaks a foreign language!

RIKKI PATEL

Every good team needs someone to take care of the "adult" jobs: staying on schedule, getting receipts, watching the budget, etc. Team Xtreme business manager Rikki handles these responsibilities with a hyper energy that sometimes drives his teammates crazy.

Rikki used to manage rock bands, so he has lots of experience with out-of-control situations. Still, he prefers calm and quiet to the sort of wildness that often follows Team Xtreme. He's a nervous person who gets queasy on a merry-go-round, but he still seems to get caught in the middle of every extreme chase and maneuver.

Rikki is driven, ambitious, and a master promoter. He is the one who came up with Alex's nickname, "Action Man." Rikki is trusted by Alex and the rest of the Team for his honesty and skills.

 Thanks to Rikki, Big Air is stocked to the gills with airsick bags...all with the Action Man logo on them, of course!

Once they finished looking over their data files, the Team brought each other up to speed.

"Looks like our files are all clean so far," Grinder reported.

Rikki had an idea. "Wait a minute, what about Simon Grey? What do we really know about him. . . ?"

"You can't be serious," Alex said. "He's one of the good guys!"

"Well, he's definitely into all that double-secret super-spy stuff," Rikki said. "I'm just saying. . . ."

"I'll go meet Simon in person to see what he knows," Alex said. "You guys keep looking. Check our equipment files next."

TEAM XTREME EQUIPMENT

<< MODULAR ARMOR
The Modular Armor can adapt to almost any extreme situation in an instant. By adding or subtracting snap-on parts, Alex is set for action on ice, water, rough terrain, or even mid-air.

LUGE SUIT >>
The Luge Suit makes the sled a part of Alex's body, so he can make the fastest possible downhill runs.

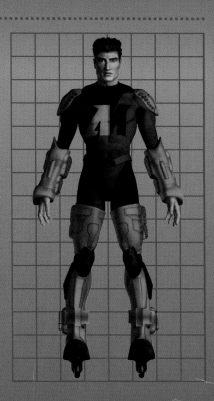

<< GLIDER PACK
While at rest, the Glider Pack is a compact backpack. But it can also spring open to a 10-foot wingspan, so Alex can soar in the air with great control.

I've updated the Modular Armor to operate by remote control, so it can work even without anyone actually wearing it. That way, the bad guys think they're chasing Alex when they're actually chasing no one.

TEAM XTREME EQUIPMENT

 I added a custom motor and advanced mountain-bike wheels. You can roll over anything from loose rocks to sand with this thing!

^^ MOUNTAIN BOARD
The Mountain Board is a motorized morph of an old-style skateboard. It can work on almost any terrain.

<< WIND BOARD
The Wind Board is a standard board-and-sail setup, but it also has hidden wheels for surfing on land.

BIG AIR

Big Air is Team Xtreme's headquarters and home away from home. It has everything the Team needs for competing on the Acceleration Games circuit. It also has special features added by Grinder for crime fighting, such as snowmobiles and jetskis.

See also LITTLE AIR.

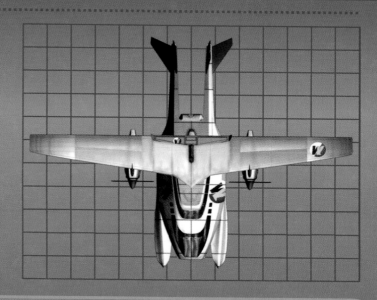

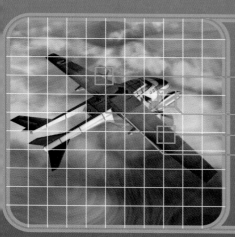

- Twin, pivoting propellers for VToL ("Vertical Takeoff and Landing")
- Pontoons for water and ground landings
- Super-strong light-alloy materials
- Three-level interior
- Detachable ultralite jet: LITTLE AIR

 The half-pipe ramp formed by the wings is great for wing-boarding.

 These VtoL propellers, which let Big Air go straight up, also work great for creating a powerful updraft for windboard practice sessions!

LITTLE AIR

Little Air is attached to BIG AIR and can separate to fly on its own. Little Air includes an in-flight camera and braking grapnel. Also, while only Grinder pilots Big Air, Little Air can be flown by everyone on the Team except Rikki.

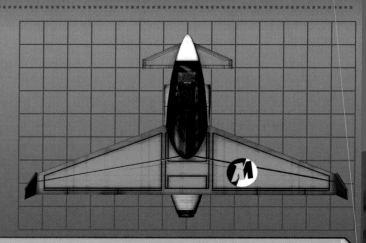

 Since I know someone will ask, the braking grapnel is a hook and line that shoots out to help Little Air stop quickly in emergencies.

HELICOPTER

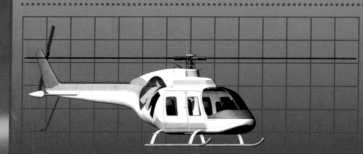

Though BIG AIR is Team Xtreme's main air vehicle, the Team also has access to this hopped-up 'copter for times when they need to get in close.

HELMET CAM

The Helmet Cam, also know as "Fidget Cam," is specially designed to be used hands-free. Fidget gets right in the middle of the action, and the camera captures everything she sees. No one knows what the rubber duckie on top is for, but Fidget insists that it remain.

 The duckie is VERY important and that's all anyone needs to know. Now mind your own business!

SILVER SPEEDER

 SECURE

Alex's sports car is constantly being improved by Grinder. Its newest feature is a rope-and-grapple firing device for special stunt performances.

"It looks like our equipment files are safe and sound," Grinder reported.

"I hope Alex can get answers from that old Simon Grey," Fidget said. "He should be close to the meeting place by now."

Meanwhile, aboard Little Air, Alex quickly
checked Simon Grey's file on the computer.

SIMON GREY

 🔒 SECURE

Simon Grey is a mysterious man. He used
to be a member of the top secret
organization PROJECT PHOENIX, which was
considered a failure and broke up after
the government cut its budget.

Simon Grey has been watching over Alex
Mann ever since Alex began showing signs
of the AMP Factor. Simon helps from the
shadows and often in secret.

 Can you imagine how weird it
would be if you found out that
one of your teachers at school
was actually a member of a top
secret agency, which was spending
millions of dollars to study you? To
tell you the truth, it was creepy to
find out I was a guinea pig! I guess
I'm lucky that Simon decided to tail me
after Project Phoenix broke up, because
another member of that organization was
Dr. X, and he's just plain bad. Simon
can be mysterious, and I never know
when or where he's going to show up,
but he's helping me learn how to unlock
the AMP Factor so I can use it better.

Before long, Alex was on the ground in the desert many miles away. This was
the secret place where Simon had asked him to come for their meeting.

"You called?" a voice asked. It was Simon Grey, who seemed to appear out of nowhere.

Alex explained the situation. "So, I have to ask: Are you the one hacking our computers?"

"You were right to come to me," Simon answered. "I'm not your man, but I do have something that will help you track the one who is."

Back on Big Air, the rest of the Team kept searching the computer files.

"Actually, I did see something in Simon Grey's file," Grinder said. "My security software says that the hacker spent quite a bit of time trying to get into his file, as if he wanted the information badly."

"None of the other athletes would care or even know about Simon Grey," Rikki said, "so they wouldn't try his file. That means. . . ."

"That means we're dealing with one of the bad guys," Grinder offered.

"No problem," Fidget said, patting her pet lizard. "Let's just figure out who it is and I'll sic ol' Vinnie here on them!"

Alex returned from his meeting with Simon. "Hey guys, you'll like what I have for you," he said. He handed Grinder a small computer chip.

"What is it?" Fidget asked.

"Simon says it contains the 'digital footprints' of all agencies and organizations on both sides of the law," Alex explained.

"This is great!" Grinder said as he examined the small device. "I can use this to see exactly who keeps trying to get into our files—if I can get it to work."

"And can you?" Rikki asked.

"No worries!" Grinder answered. "It just might take a while to load up."

"In the meantime, let's look at the guy who should have been our main suspect all along," Rikki said. "The baddest of them all—Dr. X!"

Alex agreed as he got Dr. X's file on the screen.

DR. X

 SECURE

DR. X was once a member of PROJECT PHOENIX, along with SIMON GREY. Dr. X works on improving human abilities, but does not care how many people he hurts along the way. He feels that his goal of a better human race is worth whatever it takes to get there.

One of Dr. X's failed experiments resulted in his current scarred condition. Now he must wear a mask to help him breathe. The lower half of his body is a cyber-mechanical wheelchair-like machine.

 DR. X is creepy looking, creepy sounding, just plain creepy! And to think we actually had to help him once when his Trilobytes went out of control. I don't remember a thank-you from him!

Dr. X is a brilliant scientist. Since his accident, he has been able to make himself more dangerous and powerful by conducting experiments on himself.

Dr. X is helped by insect-like Trilobytes. These are robot drones that do just about everything for him. They can also attach to his mechanical lower half to form extra tools and limbs.

Supersmall Nano-Trilobytes (NTBs) are microscopic versions of his robo-bugs that can invade and control computers and machines. Dr. X is working toward a version of NTB that can infest human beings.

 I've noticed that Dr. X is becoming less and less human as he does more and more experiments on himself. It's affecting his brain, and he's seriously tweaked. He's now able to "morph," or "change," and is much stronger than he ever was before. We've also seen him use a robotic arm, and cybernetic headgear that seems to produce earpieces and surveillance lenses as he needs them.

"It was a good idea, but it's not Dr. X," Grinder reported. "I've got Simon's chip installed and I checked Dr. X's digital signature first. No match."

"Well, how about some of his monkey-squad henchmen?" Fidget offered. "I think Brandon Caine would try something like this, especially if it meant messing up Alex during a race!"

"Fidget has a point," Rikki agreed. "He's disappeared, but we still aren't sure how or where. Let's check him out!"

BRANDON CAINE

Brandon Caine was one of ALEX MANN's closest friends, as well as his closest competition in extreme sports events. Caine was getting tired of finishing second to Alex. Dr. X told Caine he could make him faster and stronger and convinced him to try some implants.

At first, Dr. X's implants worked. Caine became an unstoppable athlete. But before long, the experiment began to fail. When Caine's adrenaline pumped up, he would lose control and turn into a wild, hulkish creature.

Caine started working with Dr. X to control his implants and change how he looked. He became a master of disguise without the help of makeup. But then Caine mysteriously disappeared. His whereabouts are still unknown.

 I never want to have to fight Brandon. But when he's out of control and under Dr. X's power, my friends are in danger and I have to stop him. I still believe we'll be able to find Brandon and cure him.

 Alex is such a softy! Brandon was jealous and bad news. We're better off now that he's missing and not able to help Dr. X anymore!

"No match there, either," Grinder said. "Next?"

"Try Asazi," Alex offered. "She's always trying to impress her boss, Dr. X. This might be one of her special projects."

"I think she'd like to impress you," Fidget said with a grimace. "She's done everything but send you flowers!"

"Less yakking and more working," Rikki warned. "Bring up her file."

ASAZI

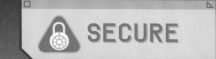

Little is known about Asazi beyond the fact that she is a one-woman terrorist squad. She will work for anyone, good or bad, for money. She is a master of high-tech weapons and hand-to-hand combat. Asazi seems to like Alex, however, which has helped ruin her plans in the past.

 If we could just get Alex to flirt with Asazi a little, maybe she'd come on over to our side!

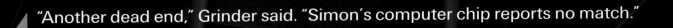

"Another dead end," Grinder said. "Simon's computer chip reports no match."

"How about Tempest?" Alex asked.

"He's a boy-wonder sort of guy who would like to show us and Dr. X how smart he is," Grinder replied. "He could do something like this. I'll run his file."

"Yeah, that crazy weather boy really drives me crazy!" cried Fidget. "I'd love to show him who's boss."

TEMPEST

Before an accident transformed him, Temple Storm was a 16-year-old boy genius. He developed technology that could control the weather. Now, as Tempest, he is able to create lightning bolts at will and is looking for revenge against people like NICK MASTERS, whom he blames for his accident. Tempest has a floating "airship" base that he can make invisible, which Dr. X also uses.

"Tempest is a very, very smart kid, but Simon's computer chip says he's not our guy," Grinder sighed. "Wait a minute. . . ."

"What do you see?" Alex asked.

"I was working ahead and checking files that might have been hacked," said Grinder, "and there's one that's been hit over and over again. The hacker keeps knocking at the door, but my security software won't let her in."

"Her?" Rikki asked.

"Yup," said Grinder. "I think we're being tested by the grownups at InterCEPT."

INTERCEPT

SECURE

International Council for the Elimination and Prevention of Terrorism, an official organization with offices all over the world.

DIANA ZERVAX

SECURE

Zervax is a tough-as-nails agent for InterCEPT. She often meets Team Xtreme when they get involved in the same investigation. Zervax thinks Team Xtreme is a group of "beginners," and she doesn't like working with them. Diana Zervax has armed forces and secret service training. She is very disciplined, the exact opposite of easygoing Fidget and Grinder.

Zervax has slowly learned to accept Alex Mann's unique abilities and she appreciates his dedication. She is beginning to accept him as a fellow professional.

When we first met Zervax, she tried to arrest Alex on some bogus charges when Brandon Caine was running around pretending to be Alex. That sure wasn't good for PR, and she didn't believe us when we said Alex was innocent. We could have avoided lots of trouble if Zervax could just lighten up!

It was terrible being blamed for things I didn't do, but Diana actually saw me breaking the law. How could she know she was really seeing Brandon, who had morphed into an exact copy of me?

"We have a match, and she's online right now!" Grinder announced. "Should I send her a small surprise?"

"Absolutely," Alex said. "Then shut down her access. I'd say we passed her little security exam!"

Miles away, in InterCEPT headquarters, Diana Zervax was startled to see a message fill her screen:

"THERE'S A BIG SPIDER ON YOUR SHOULDER."

She barely resisted checking herself before another message appeared:

"GOTCHA!"

Diana smiled. "Maybe they're ready for the big leagues after all," she said to herself.

Marketing Manager: Ali T. Kokmen
Editor: Julie Mazur
Designer: New York Zoom, Inc.
Production Manager: Hector Campbell
Text set in 14 pt. U55 and 11 pt. 2160Nickel

First published in 2001 by
Watson-Guptill Publications,
770 Broadway, New York, NY 10003
www.watsonguptill.com

Library of Congress Control Number: 2001091047

Printed in the United States of America

First printing, 2001

1 2 3 4 5 6 7 8 / 08 07 06 05 04 03 02 01

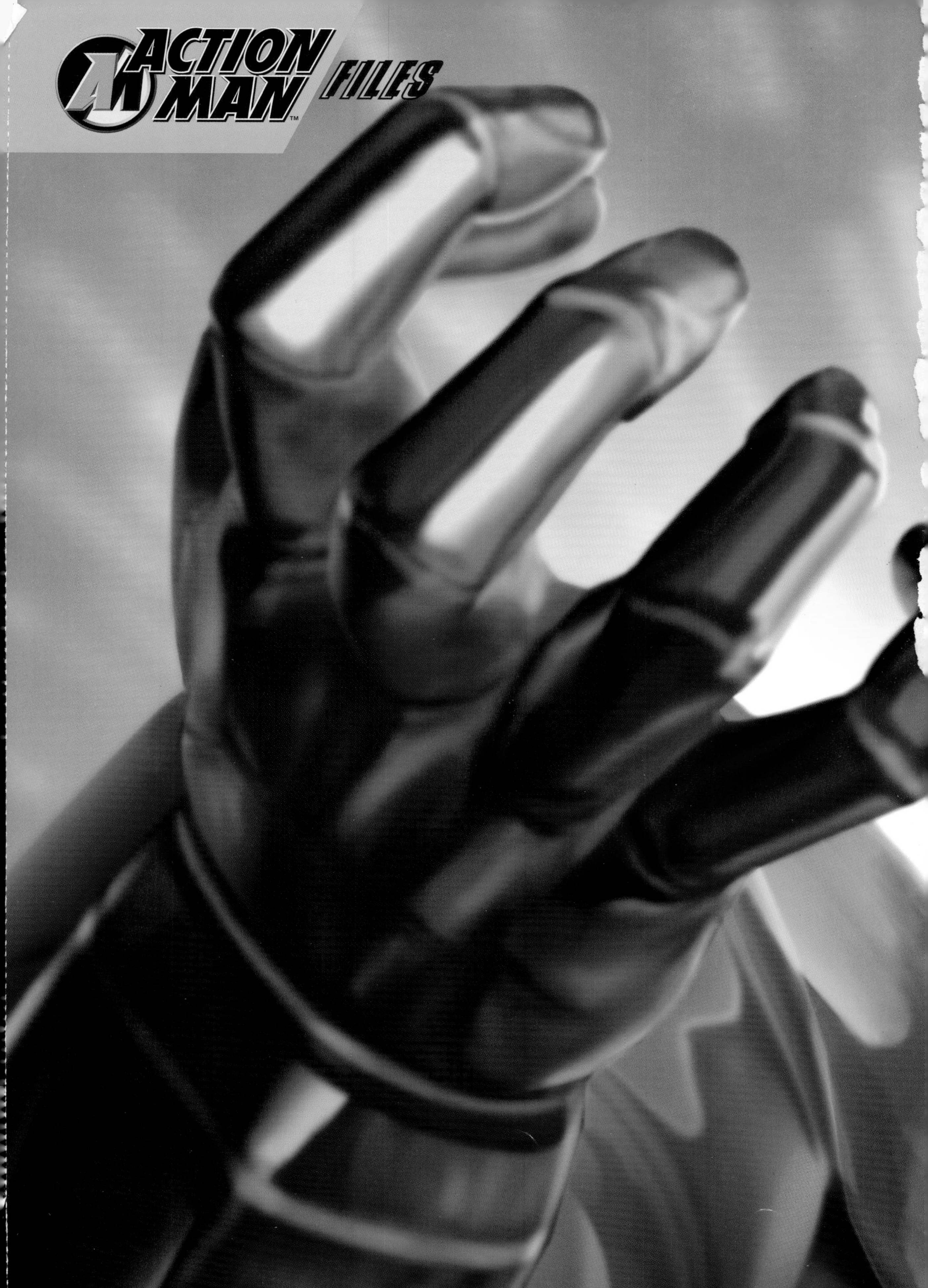
ACTION MAN FILES